NEGOTIATIONS

NEGOTIATIONS

EARTH'S SECRET ALLIANCE
RYAN WILCOX: EPISODE 1

TONY B. RICHARD

Disclaimer: Extreme vegetarianism mentioned. The topic may not be suitable for all ages. Parental Guidance is suggested.

Third Edition, October 2025

Cover designed by Perky Visuals
Interior designed & edited by Carolin Petersen
Titles typeset in Kallisto

ISBN 978-1-0698372-0-2 (paperback, regular)
ISBN 978-1-7781914-0-4 (ebook)

visit *www.tonybrichard.com*

Dedicated to my wife Lydia, and my family who have been very supportive throughout this process.

Also dedicated to those who have known self-doubt in their lives and those who have struggled to see the other side of things.

TABLE OF CONTENTS

CHAPTER ONE

AN UNEXPECTED CALL

SOMEWHERE IN NEW MEXICO

July 14, 1947

"You want me to make an alliance with aliens? Did I hear that right?" Ryan couldn't have been more shocked.

Two days earlier...

Ryan Wilcox tilted his head from side to side, dabbing thick foam across his cheeks, his usual morning ritual. Standing in front of the mirror in the bathroom of his one-bedroom apartment, the usual hustle and bustle of New York carried on outside his window. He set down the brush and flipped open his razor, slid the blade with practiced ease through the shaving lather.

The day wasn't unusual. Overcast, thick clouds painted the city in gray tones. It probably would rain later into the afternoon, but for now, the streets were dry.

He patted his cheeks and applied aftershave, then set out into the kitchen, expecting the kettle to be whistling for his morning coffee. A shrill ring filled the living room instead. With a sigh and a longing glance at his comic book and empty mug, he took the handset off the wall.

"Hello?"

A deep voice crackled over the line. "Mr. Wilcox?"

Ryan's heart raced, and he nearly dropped the phone. "Mr. President?" he asked.

"Yes," the president replied in a serious, professional tone. "I have an important ambassador position for you and your assistant."

The president has a position for me! Wait.... "What?" His voice cracked, his throat suddenly dry. Swallowing, he hurried to answer. "I mean, thank you. But I thought you said I'm too young for anything big."

The president cleared his throat, which sent a wave of static over the line, like someone crumpling paper into the mouthpiece. "Yes…. Well…. This is a unique situation. Top secret. You won't be able to tell your friends or family where you are going. Are you OK with that?"

"Um…. Yes sir, but where am I going?" Ryan asked.

"There's not much I can disclose over the phone, but know that should you accept, you'll be negotiating with a foreign government. They are currently under siege, and they need our help to defend themselves. I'll have a car pick up you and your assistant on Monday morning to take you to the airport."

Ryan nodded, then realized the president couldn't see him. "Yes, sir! Thank you, sir!"

Without even a reply from the president, the line went dead. Ryan stared at it a moment as the raspy dial tone buzzed from the receiver, much like the buzzing in his own head.

What could be so important that the president would call on a Saturday? He couldn't help but picture himself being escorted through the unmarked hallways of a secret military base, or perhaps being driven to an obscure location by men in suits. "And where am I going?" he asked aloud to the room. No one answered, obviously, as he lived alone.

Just then, the kettle shrieked, and he almost tripped over the twenty-five-foot coiled phone cord as he dashed to the kitchen and turned the burner off. Grabbing the steamy wooden handle of the kettle, almost burning himself, he moved it on to a cool burner. The whistling stopped.

The phone in his hand still buzzed with the raspy dial tone. *The president is sending a plane for me and my assistant on Monday. I should probably let Donna know.* Sticking his fingers into the dial, he spun it in the familiar pattern of her number.

CHAPTER TWO

ON A HOT DESERT HIGHWAY

SOMEWHERE IN NEW MEXICO
July 14, 1947

"You want me to make an alliance with *aliens*? Did I hear that right?" Ryan couldn't have been more shocked if General Jones had dressed up like a rubber chicken drenched head to toe in iced lemonade.

Not that the general seemed like the type to do that. Ryan recognized him, but only in passing. A friend of his father's, most likely.

The man was high-ranking, too. Four stars gleamed upon his suit. His hair was graying, so Ryan guessed he was in his later years, sixties maybe, but his shoulders kept the broad strength of a soldier in his prime. And the strength Jones carried was of one completely in his element. Ryan couldn't help but envy him.

Ryan's assistant, Donna Warren, sat next to him, her legs crossed daintily and her hands in her lap over his traveling briefcase. A black man in sleek glasses drove, a young soldier by the looks of his buzz cut and faded green uniform.

They were sitting in the back of a black stretched limo, not one of those ugly green army ones a general usually rode in. The two rear bench seats faced each other. *This must really be important.*

They were driving through what Ryan could only describe as the middle of nowhere. Realistically, he knew they were somewhere between the Albuquerque Municipal Airport and their unknown destination, but when he looked out the window, he only saw dirt, sand, and a few green shrubs.

Jones leaned forward, gaze steady. "Yes."

The word snapped Ryan's attention back to the man across from him.

"You *must* be joking!" But the seriousness in Gen. Jones's tone and the firm set of his face told Ryan that he wasn't. "How do I form an alliance with an alien race?"

"How did you negotiate the peace treaties?"

The familiar weight of self-doubt settled in Ryan's chest as he cringed. "...I didn't. I gave my suggestions to the older and more competent men. They are the ones who negotiated the treaty!" *How could anyone think that I'd done all that? I'm only twenty-six!*

"I disagree. Yes, they did the negotiations, but they used your work. I'd say none are more competent than you, Wilcox. You are the son of one of the *best* ambassadors we have, but this requires a younger perspective." The general smiled.

Ryan caught a twinkle in the general's eyes. *Oh no, what did my dad say?*

"Your father tells me you've been negotiating since you learned how to talk. He says your mother could never say no to you about anything."

"I can vouch for that," Donna said, jumping in with a matching twinkle. She grinned with the same smugness of a cat eyeing a vat of cream. "Well…since middle school, anyway. I helped him practice for the debate team. There wasn't an argument he couldn't win."

Flashes of endless afternoons spent together played behind his eyelids like a film at the cinema. "Yes, but—"

Jones interrupted him. "You learned several foreign languages and cultures from your father's placements. You have a master's degree in politics." He paused. "Yes, you were a junior negotiator when you started, but you worked your way up, and the only things keeping you from being called senior negotiator are your babyface and your age."

A pinch of annoyance raced down Ryan's spine at the mention of the familiar nickname. *How'd I get stuck with Babyface, anyway?* He shook himself.

"The president himself has noticed how hard you've worked, and the senior members of your team recommended you for an ambassador position when you're older."

Ryan's eyebrows shot up. "They *did*? They didn't tell me that. —But that doesn't change anything! In Paris, I was one of many. Who do I have now?" *I can hardly negotiate an alliance with an alien race without a team. Are there more negotiators already at their base, or am I going in alone?*

Donna gave an exaggerated gasp. "*Um!*"

Ryan barely glanced at her. He looked back at Jones, hoping to find all the answers in the man's lined face.

"In Paris, you were negotiating with multiple countries. Obviously, we can't bring in a lot of people on this. You've mentioned several times that you want an ambassadorship. This is the only way you are going to get one at your age. Your multicultural experience and love of space and science fiction makes you uniquely qualified for the job. The president and I thought you would *jump* at the chance." Jones sighed.

Ryan suddenly felt sick. *What if I fail? What would that say about me—about my father?* He couldn't blow his first big chance. "I need more time to think it over. Is it possible for me and Donna to speak in private?"

"Sure," the general said. He glanced over his shoulder through the divider window. "Corporal Dow, stop the car, please."

The black man, now known to Ryan as Cpl. Dow, eased the limo to the side of the road. The moment it stopped, Ryan threw open the door and stepped out.

"Let's go for a walk," he said, holding the door for Donna. Beyond seeing one of her feet leave the car, he didn't wait. He was already walking away at a quick pace, hands sweaty and shaking. Only subconsciously did he register Donna's hurried footsteps behind him, and her grunts and grumbles about the desert.

He didn't even speak for the first ten minutes, lost in his own head. Then, he turned to her and felt a spark of guilt at seeing her ruffled form, but brushed it aside and asked, "So, what do you think?"

Donna threw her hair back. Ryan could tell she hadn't been expecting to walk anywhere. She wore a yellow dress and cream-colored heels—he winced at the thought of her keeping up with him in those. She would wear an outfit like that to the office, not trekking across the desert. At least she'd left his briefcase in the car. No need for her toting *that* around on top of everything.

"I was as shocked as you were at first," she admitted, "but it does sound interesting, and I think you're well suited to it."

"Well suited to negotiate with aliens?" He gaped at her.

"You know what I mean."

Yes, he did. They'd been friends for over twelve years now, and she knew him better than anyone else. Ryan sighed and kept walking, a little slower this time. "How am I supposed to negotiate with aliens? It's never been done before."

"If anyone can do it, you can," Donna assured him.

It wasn't until she grabbed his hand that he realized it was still shaking. Her nails were painted a shade of red to match her lipstick.

"Maybe…." He thought about it, turned the assignment over in his head a few times. A fresh wave of worry washed over him, filling his gut with dread.

Nope! he told himself. *Too many things could go wrong. The senior negotiators are right. This is too much for me right now.* "No. I'm sure there's someone else better suited to the job. I'm far too young to be the only one on this assignment!"

Donna frowned at him, annoyed, but then her face turned into a reassuring smile. "You won't be alone; you have me, and we've been an unstoppable team since our first year together, remember?" She locked elbows with him.

"I guess we *do* make a great team." He hummed softly.

"Of course we do," Donna said. "Remember our junior year when we practiced every afternoon, so you'd be prepared to face Theo Turner in the school's debate tournament finals?"

"Yes," Ryan said.

"So…will you take the position?"

"This is a big step. I don't think they'll accept me." He pulled away from her and stalked forward again, hands gesturing wildly in the air. "No one *ever* takes me seriously! You know what it's like. In school, we were all the same age, but in the real world, no matter how good you are, they'll always take it better from an older man!"

"Listen to yourself. All I'm hearing is you flapping your lips, and you know what's coming out? Bupkis. If you're trying to argue your way out of this, know that I know all your tricks!" Her hands were in the air, too—in exasperation. "Maybe you should grow a beard, so they don't call you Babyface."

Ryan stared at her for a moment, mouth agape. He rubbed his chin. *Is that why they call me that?* "Maybe," he said. "But I'm not a rebel."

Donna nodded sharply, then groaned. "I can't go any further with these shoes." She lifted one of her feet to rest it, shifting her hips.

Ryan winced in sympathy as he looked at her shoes again. A quick glance at his wristwatch told him they'd been walking for half an hour. Half of that, he wasn't even talking! He felt the need to apologize, but it wouldn't do much about her foot pain. "So, you think I should do it?" he asked her again, just to make extra sure.

Donna stared at him incredulously. She tipped her chin down in another affirmative nod. Ryan took that as a 'yes'.

"OK, you convinced me," he said, ignoring Donna's sigh. He laughed. "Maybe *you* should be the ambassador."

"Very funny, wise guy." Donna shifted her weight to the other foot, nearly stumbling over. She caught herself on his shoulder. "Do you think they can bring the car? I don't think I can walk that far back."

Ryan twisted back around to face the limo, which happened to be considerably harder with Donna hanging off him. "We need a ride!" he shouted across the desert.

He saw Cpl. Dow raise two hands to cup his mouth. The man must've been yelling, but Ryan couldn't hear. "They are not getting into the car. They must not want to drive on the desert sand. I guess I wasn't thinking when I bolted out of the car. We should have gone along the road." Ryan sighed. "It looks like we are going to have to walk back. Here, take my shoes; it's the least I can do for making you walk all this way." He knelt down on the ground to unlace his shoes, feeling the hot sand burning through the fabric of his pants.

"Your shoes won't fit me, but thanks."

Ryan tied his shoe back up, and they were walking back when the landscape shimmered, and he swayed, a little dizzy. The desert around them continued to blur—like a mirage. For a moment, Ryan wondered if they'd been out in the sun too long, and if he got heatstroke. He'd had it before—once, as a kid. He didn't remember much from the experience, only that it *wasn't* like this. For one, neither he nor Donna had been slurring their words through that entire conversation, nor did he feel confused.

Another step forward, and suddenly they were somewhere else. His head throbbed, blood rushed through his ears, and his stomach felt like it had decided to take a vacation down to his left ankle. But that wasn't the weirdest thing. Not at all.

A bald man, mauve in color, stood right in front of him, wearing a funny foil robe. Another man, this one bright blue, sat at a floating desk, staring out at the desert through a window. Donna gasped, so at least Ryan knew he wasn't the only one going crazy. *Oh,* he thought, *these must be the aliens.*

To be fair, when Gen. Jones said *alien,* Ryan hadn't been expecting them to look like this. As much as they didn't look like they belonged on Earth, the men in front of him could've just been bald, short humans covered head to toe in body paint, but Ryan knew that wasn't the case. The way he held himself so confidently told Ryan *exactly* what he needed to know: This man wasn't from Earth, and they were on a—*spaceship?*

The mauve alien stepped forward. Ryan thought he must've been about Gen. Jones's age, but the only indicator of such were the deep lines in his face. He had no hair, and everything about him was mauve—his skin, his lips, his eyes. "You asked for a ride?"

Ryan noticed that the alien's teeth, which were exposed when he spoke, were familiar and white. He felt himself nodding, and glanced at Donna, whose mouth had dropped open, so he snapped his own shut.

The mauve alien nodded and turned to the other alien. Through the window, Ryan could see the desert landscape fly by in a blur, and suddenly they were at the limo. Jones and Dow were back in the vehicle, and it drove forward, but the spaceship they were in passed them and lowered to the ground.

A few seconds later, the blue alien tapped his desk a few times and said something in a foreign language. *"They are on board,"* the computer translated. Then he rose and turned to them, bending forward at the waist in a formal bow.

"I welcome you to the bridge of the *Ymit*. Ymit, in your language, means Hope. I am Captain Agugua. It is an honor to have you with us." Unlike the purple one, he had a deep and thick accent that Ryan couldn't decipher. His words were stilted, like some foreigners he'd heard speaking English in the past.

Ryan bowed. "Thank you. We're glad to be here."

Agugua returned to his seat. The ship began moving again, startling Ryan once more with how fast and smoothly they moved.

The purple alien spoke in a light tone. "Mr. Wilcox, Miss Warren, I am Ambassador Geogram. It is a pleasure to meet you." He bowed to them.

Not knowing what else to do, Ryan and Donna returned the bow.

"You might feel a little dizzy after walking through the very strong electromagnetic field that makes us invisible." Geogram paused for a moment.

Ryan felt like he couldn't breathe. His pulse quickened in fear.

Geogram raised his forehead and quickly added. "No need to worry; short-term exposure does not harm you in any way."

Ryan sighed. *That's a relief,* he thought and glanced around the ship. The captain said they were on the bridge, but Ryan couldn't figure out how he flew the ship by tapping his desk. It didn't look like the bridge of any ship he'd been on before. More like a classroom, though the desks and chairs were magically floating.

Ryan turned to Geogram. "Pardon me for saying so, but you speak English better than I expected. I've been to many foreign countries, and I have to say, I can't even hear an accent." He couldn't help his eyes wandering to the captain as he said this. If the ambassador could speak fluent English, that certainly put some of his worries at ease.

"Thank you. I have been listening to your radio transmissions and watching your television for many years. The rest of the crew learned to speak it on our journey here." Geogram extended a hand toward Agugua. "Except for our dear captain, who said he is too old to learn a new language."

Agugua turned briefly with a smirk. The desert blur in the windshield became an army basecamp with several tents and army vehicles spread out before them.

Ryan saw a line of army vehicles on one side next to a large barracks tent and a training field. Some soldiers were out doing drills, and Ryan's heart went out to them for exercising in this heat.

"Welcome to Area Two." Geogram smiled as he held his hand toward the ship's pocket door, which opened on its own. Ryan and Donna stepped out onto the ground.

The temporary nausea wasn't that bad the second time, and it sure beat walking. However, when Ryan turned back to the ship, his jaw dropped. There was no ship. So he reached out, then jumped back in surprise when his hand vanished right off the end of his arm. *Holy—!*

Donna tapped his shoulder and pointed to the nose of the general's limo appearing out of nowhere. The rest appeared as it drove off the ship. Ryan heard something pathetic, a few gasping syllables, and it took a few seconds before he realized the sounds were coming from him.

The limo parked, and Jones stepped out, the corners of his lips upturned in amusement. "Mr. Wilcox."

Ryan snapped his mouth shut again and composed himself. He looked at Donna, who looked back at him, her lips pursed in thought. He knew this expression well. She always did it when unsure about something. Unsure, but excited. Ryan smiled at her.

"This ought to be fun. Are you ready?" he asked.

Donna nodded, and they took the first step toward the general.

CHAPTER THREE

BRIEFING

EARTH–ZALMA BASECAMP, NEW MEXICO

Gen. Jones seemed completely in his element, despite wearing a neatly pressed suit out in the middle of nowhere. The Area Two basecamp wasn't much to look at. Just a few tents, one nearby marked for Jones to use as his office. Cpl. Dow had gotten out of the car as well and stood next to Jones, who Ryan noticed carried his leather briefcase.

"Did you enjoy your ride?" Jones asked as they approached.

Is that a teasing smirk? I never expected to see General Jones acting so casual! Maybe the startled look on my face is more amusing than I thought. "Was I…." Ryan began, only for Donna to glare at him. He coughed. "Um, sorry…. Were *we* just on a spaceship?"

"Yes," Jones said, "how did you like it?"

"Um, it's fast! I didn't have time to enjoy it."

The general's smile widened, like he expected that answer. "So, are you in or out?"

"I'm in."

"Good. You'll need this, *Ambassador* Wilcox." Jones offered the briefcase. "Let's go talk before you meet with them. We thought you would be more comfortable negotiating on our home turf."

"*Home turf*? You mean *desert sand*." Ryan laughed lightly, trying to calm his nerves. They'd just been set on edge again. The others laughed with him, which made him feel better.

Jones took them into the military tent marked for himself. It was plain, like any old tent, with a foldout table in the middle, surrounded by four chairs, one of them occupied by another spectacled young man looking at a piece of polished metal. A cabinet sat to one side, and the table had a single beige file.

Seeing the general, the soldier pocketed the metal, stood, and saluted. "General."

Jones returned the salute. "At ease. Corporal Rabinowitz, meet Ambassador Wilcox and Miss Warren."

They greeted each other and shook hands.

Jones joined Rabinowitz on the far side of the table. Ryan and Donna took the available seats. Ryan popped open his briefcase and withdrew a notepad for Donna and several pens, which he set on the table between them. He accepted the file that Jones slid across the table for him and flipped it open, exposing about a dozen papers. Ryan scanned a page and then passed it to Donna. As a woman, she normally wouldn't even be invited to discussions like this, but he'd always thought that view was silly.

She was just as clever and skilled at debating, yet she wasn't allowed to join the team—so he tried to include her as much as possible. He knew the others in his field looked down on his methods, even his father to some extent, but he and Donna made a good team, so he kept it that way.

They were halfway through the file when the general began speaking.

"You should know a few things. First, the aliens are from a planet called Zalma, and we are calling them the Zalmen. They are pacifists, which means they know nothing about fighting. That also means they need all the help they can get against Moad—the planet that's attacking them."

Jones was silent for a while, so when Ryan finished the page, he looked up and nodded.

Jones continued. "In exchange for our help, they'll be giving us their technology and teaching us how to use it. Obviously, their technology is very advanced. They have no weapons, but I'm sure that our people can re-purpose their tools into weapons so we can defend Earth."

Beside him, Donna scribbled away in shorthand at a speed Ryan couldn't even hope to accomplish. "Not that I would imagine doing this, but what's stopping us from taking their technology and not helping them?"

"The same thing that tells me that you are not serious," Rabinowitz said. He tapped his glasses. "Zalmen technology can detect things like lying and hatred. They gave us these glasses to help us recruit people who are safe."

Ryan's heart thudded with excitement. "Really? There is technology in those glasses?"

"Yes, and in this communicator." Rabinowitz pulled out the polished metal rectangle he'd been fidgeting with as they'd walked in. Ryan got a closer look. It was small and slightly bigger than a playing card, and the notion that it could be used in any way similar to Ryan's home rotary phone was almost unbelievable.

Donna leaned forward. Her eyes flashed with curiosity. "How does it work?"

"Voice commands. *Communicator, show me the list.*"

Donna, who'd reached for the device on the table, drew her hand back with a mild gasp of surprise as words appeared on its sleek surface.

Ryan saw it had a list of names, some of which were crossed out and others with small check marks next to them. He recognized his own at the very top. "If this tiny thing is a communicator, could they be listening to us right now?"

Rabinowitz shrugged. "They could, but Geogram assured me that this one will only respond to me."

"And you know that he is telling the truth from the glasses that he gave you?" Ryan guessed.

"Well, I didn't have the glasses yet, but he didn't change color when he originally told me." He paused, frowning. "No…wait. He turned white, but he was probably worried because I accused him of spying on me."

"Wait, wait…*change color*?"

"Yes, that's how they evolved into a peaceful society, or so he tells me," Rabinowitz said.

"How's that?"

"I don't know the specifics, but their color shows their emotional state. Red and yellow indicate anger. I think one of them blushed, so I am not sure what that means."

Ryan leaned back in his seat, tapping his fingers on the table thoughtfully. "We turn red when we're angry or embarrassed, too. More blood flows to the skin, and it turns red, so, I would guess in both cases it is an emotional response, good or bad. But I don't know how the yellow fits in."

"And the greenish ones are scientists," Jones said, matter-of-factly. "They also become greener when they're thinking."

Ryan frowned. *So much for having that figured out.* "Thinking is not an emotion," he said. "And we saw a blue man on the ship. What does *blue* mean?"

"You said yellow indicates anger, correct?" Donna asked, looking at Rabinowitz, who nodded. "Well, in the theater, when they want to create yellow lights, they mix red and green."

"So, angry means they're emotional, as indicated by the red; and thinking, as indicated by the green," Ryan guessed. *That could work. And if that's true, then....* His mind cycled through the possibilities.

The general, however, didn't seem as impressed. "How does that help us with *blue?*"

"Simple," Donna said. "It's not there." She grinned to herself, but when she saw the blank expressions of all three men around her, she had to stop herself from rolling her eyes. "When lighting, there are three primary colors: red, green, and blue."

Ryan understood. "So, you're saying that when he is angry, he has no blue."

"Possibly."

"So, blue might indicate tranquility, peace, or something like that?" Jones asked.

"It's possible. Why don't we just ask them?" Ryan looked at Rabinowitz. Clearly, he knew the most out of all of them.

"I already did," Rabinowitz admitted. "They said it's not polite."

"Polite or not, it's my job to ask," Ryan said. "What else do I need to know?"

Rabinowitz muttered into his communicator, then spun it around so Ryan and Donna could see that the image changed to a video of a gleaming city. The sky above the city was filled with thundering explosions. Before Ryan could marvel at the clear, *colored* image,

Rabinowitz spoke. "Their planet is protected by a deflector. We would like to have them here as well."

Ryan stared at the screen, eyes wide. He leaned back, looking up at Rabinowitz again. "What else?"

"Their invisibility?"

"And we don't want to store this technology on Earth," Jones added.

"What? Why not? Where would we store it then?" Ryan asked.

"Their technology is beyond anything humans could dream of at this point. We don't want to risk it falling into the wrong hands. As for where to store it—we were thinking we'll be the only ones with spaceships, so we would like them to help us set up a base on the moon."

That, Ryan could understand. He'd seen what technology could do in the hands of bad men. He'd never been a foot soldier, never one on the front lines, but every time he heard about things happening overseas during the war.... He shuddered to think about it. "So, you want me to negotiate a moon base? What could I offer them in exchange for all this?" Awash with nervous energy again, he stood and began pacing the small tent.

"For one, you'll be going to their planet as a negotiator."

Looking the general in the eye, Ryan couldn't tell if he was serious. "I'm *what!?*"

"The president did inform you that you couldn't tell anyone where you were going, right?"

Ryan cleared his throat. "Well, yes, but I expected it to be somewhere on Earth."

"I guess we should've discussed that first. Are you OK with traveling to their planet? They want to negotiate peace with the Moadites."

Ryan leaned over his seat. "So now I'm not just negotiating with these pacifist aliens, I'm negotiating with their enemy as well!?"

Jones smiled. "Yes, but don't worry; I'm also going and bringing a team of military experts. You won't be on your own."

"Ah, so, we're trading manpower for technology?"

"Yes," Rabinowitz said. "They have brought instructors to teach us their technology. Their names are Kanara and Sarara, a married couple with two children. They're a swell family." He smiled.

"So, we are trading warriors and negotiators for teachers?" Ryan addressed Jones. "What about this moon base? What are we giving them for that?" No one spoke. "Anybody?"

"I guess you're going to have to figure that one out," the general said.

"*Great!*" Ryan grumbled. "Any *more* good news?"

Jones hummed, thinking for a moment, then shook his head. "No, I think that's it. Are you ready to meet them now?"

"No!" He wasn't. However, the others in the tent did not look impressed. He sighed. "Oh, alright." He readied himself for his first *real* conversation with an alien.

CHAPTER FOUR

NEGOTIATIONS

EARTH–ZALMA BASECAMP, NEW MEXICO

R yan had been prepared to go somewhere else for the meeting. It turned out that they were staying there in Gen. Jones's tent. He smiled to himself. *Small victories.* At least he didn't have to walk anywhere. He and Donna had moved to Jones's side of the table and were whispering together when Geogram stepped through the door with a younger lilac-colored lady at his side.

Ryan stared at her bald head for a moment. He'd never seen a bald lady before. She held herself in that elegant way that only ladies could, and her form was slimmer than Geogram's, though mostly hidden by her shapeless silver robe. Even more surprising, though, she looked to be around his and Donna's age. Donna, who must have noticed his staring, elbowed him.

"Hello again," Geogram said. He turned slightly to the lady. "Allow me to introduce our communications officer, Edugra."

Together, Ryan and Donna stood, smiling at her. "Welcome."

Both aliens bowed. *That must be how they greet each other,* Ryan thought. *Or perhaps it's just because we're being formal.* He and Donna bowed back, nonetheless. Then the four of them sat down.

Ryan shuffled his notes. He hoped to hide the fact that his hands were sweating; his heart raced in his chest. "Well…we didn't have much time to talk when you gave us a ride earlier, so I would like to welcome you to Earth." He reached across the table to offer a handshake.

Geogram accepted the handshake. "Thank you. It is an honor to meet you. We have heard great things about you, Ambassador Wilcox."

"Thank you." Ryan leaned back and adjusted his suit jacket. His hands shook for a moment longer, but then he cleared his throat. *I'm ready.* "Shall we get to it?"

Geogram and Edugra nodded.

"So, I hear you already have the basics worked out. We are providing a negotiations team, consisting of myself and Donna, and General Jones is providing a military team."

Geogram and Edugra nodded again.

"In exchange, you are providing technology, training, and a moon base. Is that right?" Ryan watched them both intently, wondering how they would respond.

Ryan knew that the moon base was not offered; he was testing their skin color theory, and as expected, Geogram and Edugra were confused. They exchanged looks, and both rapidly changed color. Ryan held back a gasp. Rabinowitz wasn't exaggerating when he said they changed—they *really* did. Geogram's skin finally settled on a sharp yellow. The lines on his face were dark and deep as he glared at Ryan across the table. "That is a lie, and you know it!"

Ryan stifled a laugh and donned his best poker face. "What am I lying about, and how do you know?"

"We did not agree to provide a moon base. Our technology tells us you are lying…." Geogram's skin turned light green. "But now I realize that you already know that, and you were testing us."

"Yes, I was," Ryan said mildly. "I have to say, if you are going to use technology on us to tell if we're lying, it's only fair if we're able to know when you're lying, too."

The light green faded from Geogram until he turned almost completely white, like someone had dusted him with flour. "You can tell our emotional state by the color of our skin."

"That's what I heard, but how does that help me? I don't know what the different colors mean. Please, enlighten me."

"It is not polite to ask," Geogram said sharply, yellow once again.

"If you won't tell me, then we aren't equal." Ryan's smile became stiff. "I refuse to continue the negotiations until the matter is resolved."

As he waited, Geogram turned yellow, then seemed to cycle through several shades of green, and flashed bright red before settling on white. Ryan tried not to stare. He kept his eyes firmly on Geogram's face. Interestingly enough, even though his skin changed, the alien's eyes stayed the same mauve that they'd been when he walked in.

"It is hard for us to speak about it," Edugra said softly, jumping in. She glanced at Geogram. "As communications officer, may I speak, Father?"

"*Father?*" Ryan asked.

Geogram nodded firmly. "Yes, Edugra is my daughter. We were observing Earth communications together, which is why we were both assigned to this mission."

They do look similar, now that I think about it. He hadn't seen it before, but now that he knew they were related, he could see that they shared some features— the roundness of their noses, the shape of their chins. He'd just replayed Geogram's words in his head when something clicked. "Wait! You were receiving our communications on Zalma? What communications?"

"Your public television and radio," Geogram said. "Why?"

"How? Those signals weren't meant to leave the city, never mind the planet."

"We have one of our probes in your orbit, relaying the signals," Edugra explained.

They're hovering in our orbit without our knowledge? Ryan tapped his pen for a few seconds. "Hmm…. Did you do the same thing to Moad? Did you spy on them, too?"

"We didn't intentionally *spy* on them, but yes, we were monitoring their public broadcasts as well," Geogram admitted.

"That's probably why they attacked you. No one likes to be watched—especially without their knowledge." His heart dropped into his stomach as a new thought suddenly occurred to him. "Were you transmitting our signals back to your planet while the Moad attacked you? Do they know where we are?"

"No! The probe would only transmit when we wanted it to, and it never did while the Moad were at our planet."

Ryan sat back. "Oh, good! Now, where were we?" His eyes wandered toward Edugra. "Ah…. You were going to tell us what your skin colors mean?"

Edugra straightened. "So, it's all fairly simple. Red is when we are emotional. Green is when we are thinking. Blue is when we are having pleasant thoughts such as home or family. Our other colors are created when we feel combinations of those."

Ryan didn't have to look at Donna to know that she was grinning. He did anyway. She was. Of course she was. She was right.

"OK, so what do yellow and white mean?" Ryan asked.

"Yellow is made up from red and green, so we are emotional and thinking. That means we are angry. White is a combination of all primary colors."

"So, you're thinking and emotional about family. In other words, you're worried. Thank you for telling us," Ryan said. The Zalmen only nodded. "One last thing—what color means you're lying?"

With a giggle, Geogram said, "Bright green. It is a dishonorable way of thinking. We do not make a habit of it. Only our young children lie, but they quickly learn that it does not work."

Surprised that Geogram had volunteered that information so freely, Ryan glanced at Edugra, who blushed. He had to remind himself that Edugra was Geogram's daughter.

"Thank you both for that. And I am sorry I got upset. Let's get back to some simple negotiations. We're willing to provide my negotiating skills and General Jones's military manpower. You're willing to provide us with technology and knowledge?"

Geogram nodded. "That is correct."

"I'm going to need numbers. How much manpower will you need, and how much knowledge will you provide?"

Geogram, who'd just gone back to his natural color, changed to cyan, then white as he considered the question. "We don't know anything about war. We don't know what we need, but we are willing to provide you with whatever you require to make the Moad stop attacking. We hope you can negotiate peace before any actual fighting occurs."

"I'll do my best. How technologically advanced are the Moad? Are they like you?" He waited, but Geogram stared at him blankly. "OK, I'll ask a simpler question. How long did it take you to get here?"

This time, Geogram answered immediately. "About five of your months."

"But there are no stars that close. You'd have to have been traveling faster than the speed of light, and that's impossible."

"Not impossible," Geogram disagreed and turned light green. "Why would you say that?"

"Einstein's theory of relativity states that nothing can travel faster than the speed of light. It's something to do with gravity."

Edugra giggled as if Ryan had said something cute. "We don't know Einstein, but we have technology that modifies what you call gravity, so those rules no longer apply."

"You can modify gravity? Holy mackerel! Good to know! Will you be teaching us this?"

"I'm certain Sarara would be willing to give a lesson on that, yes."

"So, you don't know what kind of technology the Moad have? And you don't know how long you will need our warriors, either?" Ryan looked back at

Geogram, who shook his head. "But you will provide transportation both ways, right?"

"Correct."

"So, you want us to send our warriors for five months in each direction. Let's just say it's almost a year round-trip, and they would stay for one to three years each, and then rotate home. You should probably plan for one or two trips a year. Does that sound OK?" Ryan asked.

Geogram nodded and smiled.

"So, is it safe to say that you will keep training our people on how your technology works for as long as we are protecting yours?"

"Yes. That sounds reasonable to me," the other ambassador said.

"Great, and I understand that a family will be staying on Earth to teach our people your science and technology. Kanara, Sarara, and their two children?"

"Yes."

"Great," Ryan said. "So...back to this moon base. Why don't you just give it to us?"

If Ryan expected Geogram to change color again, he was disappointed.

For the first time, Geogram's face showed no expression. "Are you testing us again? You know that is not fair, so why do you ask?"

"Because that is my job," Ryan replied. "I'm supposed to get the best deal I can for my people."

"Even when you know that it's wrong?"

"That is my job."

"Do you like your job?" Geogram inquired.

"I love my country."

"That doesn't answer my question."

"Of course it does. It's how things are done on Earth. Both sides want the best deal for themselves, and negotiations go back and forth until we settle on what's fair."

"But we are dealing with you in good faith, so what would you consider an *acceptable* trade?"

"It isn't my job to tell you what to ask for. What would you want for it?"

"What would be an equitable trade?"

Ryan felt the blood pumping through his brain, beating on his temples, trying to get out. *Does my dad ever feel like this when dealing with people? Does Geogram really not understand how to trade? Are he and his people really that content with what they have? Does Earth have that little to offer?* He turned to Donna and Edugra. "Can you help us out here?"

Edugra thought for a moment. "While my father and I were doing research, we enjoyed your radio and television shows...."

"Maybe we can work something out," Ryan suggested. He tilted his head, considering the options. "I'm sure we can get you some records. I don't think the networks would appreciate you tapping into their signals. But what about stories?"

"Entertainment is very valuable to us humans; it seems valuable to you as well. How about movies and books?" Donna suggested.

Geogram frowned. "Like home video? User manuals?"

Ryan shook his head. "No, like fiction, autobiographies, history."

"What is fiction?" Geogram asked.

"What do you mean, 'what is fiction?' Made-up stories."

"Lies?" Geogram looked and sounded aghast, emphasized by the way his entire face had turned white as a sheet.

"No, not lies. Dreams, fantasies, and entertainment. Just like on the television."

Edugra paled to match her father's white. "Do you mean the people on the television are not real?"

Ryan wasn't even sure what to say to reassure her, or what to reassure her about, so luckily, Donna jumped in. In her soothing way, she said, "Some of what you see on television is talking about real events. It's called the news. But other shows tell stories, and most of those are made from someone's imagination."

"What is imagination?" Geogram changed to green so quickly Ryan almost got whiplash.

"You don't know what imagination is either?" *How do I even explain that?* "Well, imagination is like thinking of where you will be in ten years, pretending you are the President of the United States, wondering what you'd do if you were a rich man, even flying through space! Although…that one is looking more plausible now."

Donna giggled.

"Why would you think of things that are not real?" Geogram asked.

"Sometimes to learn," Donna smiled softly. "Like Pinocchio, the wooden boy. Every time he told a lie, his nose would grow."

"How can a boy be wooden?" Edugra asked, still white, though flashes of green were rippling across her skin as well. "And how could a nose grow?"

Donna laughed. "That's the beauty of it. It's magic. *Pinocchio* is a story to teach children not to lie."

"Children's noses don't grow. They change color when they lie," Geogram said pointedly.

"Not on Earth, they don't. We don't change, so that's why we need stories like that. To show why it's wrong to lie."

"What a stimulating concept." Geogram seemed intrigued. "You mentioned magic. What is it?"

Donna leaned back in her chair, thinking. "Magic is…a supernatural power…or something that you don't understand. Most people would call your invisible ship magic."

"Our ship is not magic; it is technology."

"Most magic is just technology that we don't understand yet," Ryan said. "So, someone who doesn't know how it's possible for something to be invisible will call it magic.

"Come to think of it, doesn't the development of technology require imagination? How did you develop these technologies without imagining them first?"

"We were taught the technology." As soon as the words left his mouth, Geogram's eyes widened and his skin flashed rapidly between purple, teal, and pasty white. "Please, tell me more stories."

However, Ryan could tell when someone wanted to change the subject. "*Taught* the technology?" he pushed, frowning. "By whom?"

"That is a good question for another time," Edugra cut in.

Ryan glanced at Edugra, then back at her father. The aliens seemed nervous for some reason, not only because of their complexion, but because Ryan could see a thin trail of sweat working its way down his forehead. *They sweat? Interesting. …* Ryan wasn't a scientist at heart, but he wanted to ask.

"Please, tell me more stories," Geogram repeated.

Ryan, suspicious of the aliens' deflection about their technology, could already tell that the other ambassador would not answer. *Better to save it for later.* He wouldn't be getting that kind of answer out of him anytime soon. Instead, he looked at Donna, wondering if she had another example for the aliens. Stories had been an interest of hers since middle school.

She did. "Humpty Dumpty sat on a wall. Humpty Dumpty had a great fall. All the king's horses and all the king's men couldn't put Humpty together again." As she finished, both aliens turned indigo.

The ambassador heaved a breath. "That is a sad story."

"It's not a real story," Donna said. "It's a basic nursery rhyme."

Geogram's eyes widened, and he blinked owlishly at her. His baffled expression almost made Ryan laugh, though he stopped himself from losing his composure.

"It's to teach children that sometimes when things break, they can't be fixed," Ryan explained to the two confused aliens.

"So, you tell lies to teach your children lessons?"

"Not lies, imagination!"

There must've been *something* in Ryan's insistent tone, because Geogram seemed to be considering his words thoughtfully rather than dismissing them. He cycled through colors again, this time much faster— so fast that Ryan averted his eyes in fear of an oncoming headache.

"Do you have more examples of this *imagination*?" Geogram finally asked.

"Ah…yes, I read this on the plane." Ryan fumbled for a moment with opening his briefcase on the table to retrieve a comic book from under his business papers. The front depicted a dark-haired man in a hero suit holding up the front of a bright yellow car with one hand. The words *Adventure Comics* took up most of the top left corner, and a blocky title of 'Superman' took up the right. "And he's an alien, just like you."

Curiously and with tentative fingers, Geogram took the comic book. He flipped through it like it was a precious artifact. Then he looked up. "May I borrow this?"

"Sure."

"I believe this is an ideal time to break for the day. Here is a communicator for each of you." Geogram reached into his pocket with his free hand to retrieve two communicators and handed them over. The devices looked identical to Cpl. Rabinowitz's. "I will call you on it when I'm ready to meet next, or, if you prefer, you can ask it to call me." Then Geogram stood and left the tent, clasping the comic gently.

Ryan remained seated, unsure of what to say. He turned to Donna, but the two ladies were out of their seats and leaving the tent as well, chatting.

CHAPTER FIVE

THE ALLIANCE

EARTH–ZALMA BASECAMP, NEW MEXICO

"Ryan?" Donna called from just outside his tent. He looked up. "Come in." As Donna entered, he could see a wide grin on her face.

"I think I'm friends with an alien!" she announced.

Ryan laughed. "*Guest*," he corrected. "The general wants us to get used to us calling them *guests* so we don't slip if we are in public."

Donna ducked her head sheepishly. "Sorry, but I just had to tell someone! Edugra and I have been spending time together for the past few days—"

"Yes, I know," Ryan cut in.

"Let me finish. We've been spending time together, I just had the most wonderful conversation with her, and as I walked back it dawned on me—we're *friends*." Her grin widened. "Actually *friends*."

"I see. So what did you talk about, if you don't mind me asking?" He invited her to sit at his small table and sat himself on his cot, creasing the tight folds.

"Well, it seems as if we aren't so different after

all. We are close in age and both of our fathers are ambassadors."

"So is mine." He smirked. "All *three* of us are so similar. What else?"

"We both love listening to music and can't wait to hear each other's favorites. When Edugra and her dad listened to our radio broadcasts, she liked Doris Day and the Glenn Miller Band. And just like us, she loves 'You Are My Sunshine', though she thinks it's a little sad. Also, I showed her makeup, though *that* went belly up real quick because she kept changing color and nothing matched, so we discussed boys instead. She then told me all about Zalma, and growing up there, so I think I know what to expect when we go," Donna rattled off.

Ryan balked. "When *we* go? So, you're definitely going, then?" he asked.

"Of course, Ryan. I'm your *assistant*. Where you go, I go." She nodded firmly, leaving no room for discussion.

"Right."

Donna winked at him. "Didn't think you'd get to leave me here alone, did you? You get an ambassador-ship and suddenly you're a hotshot? I don't think so."

"But what will you tell your family?"

"What have you told yours?" she countered.

"I'm out on a top-secret negotiation and will be in

touch. My parents are used to it, but your family worries if you don't check in every other hour."

Donna shrugged. "It isn't that bad. I'll just tell my parents we're on a secret mission together. They know I'm safe when I'm with you."

Ryan sighed, but secretly, he was overjoyed that Donna was coming with him into space. He'd been in meetings with Geogram and Edugra for the past two days, same as her, but in between had managed to meet some of the other soldiers who were going and found that he had very little in common with them. All they wanted to talk about was cars, guns, sports, combat, and dames. That wasn't a surprise, but he felt better going with someone familiar. "Alright. Now, back to your bonding experience with Edugra. Anything we can use?"

"There are no gender wars on their planet—no racism. They picked mostly male leaders for this crew because they figured from our broadcasts that's what we're used to. They have just as many lady leaders as men, and the ladies don't try to be men. They lead in their own unique way. Isn't that wonderful?"

"Definitely peculiar," he replied, though he was less engaged in the conversation than earlier. His thoughts were lost in musings of space itself rather than foreign politics. He dealt with politics every day. "Anything else?" he murmured.

Donna frowned at him suddenly. "I'm not going to *spy* on her if that's what you mean, but if there is essential information that comes up, I'll let you know."

Ryan nodded. "Thanks, Donna." He paused. "Have you spoken with any of our other guests?"

Donna sighed. "Sarara's been busy with her kids, and some Cameron guy is taking over all of Joanua's time, so it's just me and Edugra. Not that I'm complaining! I like her."

Ryan felt the same. His mind flashed with images of the other two female Zalmen, then the males. None of them brought the same spark of interest he felt when he thought of Edugra. He'd have to find some time to spend with her.

The past two days were the most unusual of Ryan's entire negotiating career, perhaps even the most unusual of his entire twenty-six years of life. He wore one of his best suits, briefcase in hand, as he entered the small spaceship that came to be known as the Spacevan. Today they were going to see the president, and he would present the fruits of his first truly important assignment.

He greeted Captain Agugua, who touched his control pad a few times. Ryan saw through the windshield that the ship rose above the base camp; the landscape blurred, stopped outside Ryan's New York apartment, then blurred again, stopped at the White House, and then descended into the garden.

"Wait! I thought you were going to scan my apartment so you could duplicate it for my room on your ship."

Agugua spoke in Zalmen, and the computer translated. "*I did.*"

"Oh." Ryan then walked off the invisible ship. He scanned his surroundings, noting where he had to return to: between the red and white roses. He reached back just enough to see his hand disappear, then stood straight again.

President Whitmore called from the other side of the garden.

Ryan met him at a picnic table. "Mr. President."

Whitmore shook his hand. "Ambassador Wilcox."

Ryan put his briefcase on the table and pulled out the alliance papers. They had discussed them over the communicator, but the president wasn't one for signing something without reading it first.

Whitmore scanned the pages, occasionally pausing while his lips moved. "So, what are they like?"

"Sir?"

"What are the aliens like? I haven't met one yet." Whitmore continued to read.

"There's one in the spaceship. I can introduce you if you like."

Whitmore shook his head. "No. I trust you and Frank…sorry, General Jones. I want to be able to honestly say that *I have not met an alien* as long as possible. When the Earth Council forms, I'll meet them with the rest of the world leaders."

So he wants plausible deniability? I guess that's fair; he's under far more public scrutiny than the rest of us.

Whitmore took the pen that Ryan held for him. "Just like we discussed." Whitmore finished signing and then handed the papers back to Ryan, along with an envelope. "Please deliver this to General Jones."

Ryan smiled. "I will." He put the papers back into his briefcase and the two men shook hands. "Thank you, Mr. President."

"Thank you, Ambassador."

Ryan entered the general's tent.

Gen. Jones looked up from his paperwork. "Good morning, Ambassador Wilcox. You've been in and out of meetings for the past two days. Have negotiations been going well with our guests?"

"Yes, sir." Ryan lifted his briefcase onto the table. "They've been good, and we've signed the alliance. It's been…a unique experience, to say the least." As he spoke, he opened the case and pulled out a stack of papers: copies of the alliance. He sat and slid them forward for the general to see.

"Oh?" The general reached for them.

"Well, sir. The Zalmen do have a sense of humor, but you have to explain the joke to them." Ryan recalled the day before, when he'd walked in on Donna trying to explain the concept of *why did the chicken cross the road* to Agugua. "The jokes they tell are very dry, but that's because they have little creativity. No imagination. No sense of adventure. No fiction."

"Interesting." Jones hummed thoughtfully. "How does that help us?"

"Well, you know that entertainment is a thriving industry. On Zalma, they have no means of creating it, which is why they were retransmitting our broadcasts. They want more—more books, records, and movies. Of course, the more violent content will have to have a warning, as they are pacifists. But it's the only physical thing that we have to trade with them."

"Fascinating. So, what are we trading with them for?"

"We give them one copy of all the music and stories that have been published in our country, and they give us a space base."

"A space base? Not a moon base?" The general leaned forward, resting his elbows on the table.

"Edugra argued that if it's in space, it'll be closer to the planet, and it can be moved to help protect us. Like an aircraft carrier, but way bigger—and in space." Ryan waved his hands, trying to illustrate the size.

Jones raised a single eyebrow. "Impressive."

"If we need anything else, we will have to get more stories from other countries in the United Nations to pay for them."

Jones tilted his head. "United Nations?"

"We'll get to that later."

"OK," Jones accepted, nodding. "What about the rest of the negotiations?"

Ryan sighed and leaned back in his seat, trying to think of some highlights from the past two days of negotiations. One detail specifically stood out to him. "You know that when you and I negotiate, we usually ask for more than what we want, so that when the other person counters, we end up settling on what we originally needed?"

"Yes."

"There was none of that," Ryan informed him matter-of-factly. "I asked for what *I* thought was reasonable, and they asked for what *they* thought was reasonable. That's it! Can you believe it's only been two days? The Paris Peace Conference took almost two years!"

"Impressive!" The general's face had split into another grin. "I like these Zalmen."

"But…."

"There's always a but, isn't there?"

"You know how our laws require us to bring treaties to the Senate?"

Jones nodded knowingly. "Yes, and we can't exactly do that, can we?"

"Not unless we want the whole planet to know about them and their technology. We have to do this off the books, out of the public's eye." It had been a concern in the back of his mind for most of the first day after the main details had been hashed out. On the second day, they'd explored a few solutions, then broke for lunch, then discussed a few more. Just last night, they'd figured something out.

"Right, so what did you come up with?"

"The Earth–Zalma Alliance, or EZA for short, won't be written up as being with the US Government, but instead with the—" he made hasty air quotes "—'Peaceful Leaders of Earth'."

The general was taken aback. "Oh boy! Is the president OK with this?"

"Surprisingly, yes. I think he just wants to share the burden with the other leaders," Ryan said.

"I think you're right," Jones said. "How have you defined the Peaceful Leaders?"

"We have one year to form an Earth Defense Council and find the highest-ranking official in each country in the United Nations—safe people, of course. If we can't find a diplomat, we can recruit a military officer or a scientist. Regardless, each member should be given equal ranking on the council. Finding someone in the USSR might prove to be difficult."

"Yes," the general said with a nod and a chuckle.

"Corporals Dow and Rabinowitz have a real challenge on their hands."

"Yes, sir; they sure will. I almost forgot." He dug through his case again, this time to retrieve an envelope, which he presented with a stiff, formal posture. "I am here to officially notify you that the president has assigned you to lead a top-secret task force. Your assignment is to assemble the rest of the Earth Defense Council."

Jones shot him an incredulous look over the top of the letter. "Does the president know that I am going into space to fight aliens?"

"Yes, he does. You are to find someone to take over operations on Earth in your absence, and he is preparing a banquet for all the generals on Friday, so you and Dow can find your replacement."

Jones laughed, and jokingly he asked, "Is the president angry with me? He knows I don't like all this paperwork." He gestured to the table, with its stacks of official documents that needed reading and signing.

"I wouldn't say angry," Ryan laughed along, "but he said that he doesn't want to be seen with aliens. It would not go well for him in the next election. And he mentioned that it probably would have been easier on all of us if you'd just fired a warning shot and scared them off. But he seems to respect you and what we're doing. He just won't admit it. And I'm sure he'll also take the credit if we're successful."

Jones chuckled. "Yes, I got that impression as well. What about our security problem?"

"The treaty states we will not keep their technology on Earth, except for a minimum required for recruitment purposes and self-defense."

"And what about our personnel exchange?"

"Right." Ryan reached over the table to flip through the treaty; the general scanned the newly revealed page. "Geogram will stay as the Zalma representative. Kanara, Sarara, and their children will stay to teach our scientists while you, your specialists, and I travel to their planet to negotiate and assess the situation."

"Good work!" Jones praised him. He folded the treaty together again, then leaned back and heaved a sigh. "Now, the hard part. I have to tell my wife that I'll be gone for two or three years."

"Good luck with that, sir."

Jones eyed Ryan curiously. "By the way, your file says that you are single. Are you and Miss Warren...?"

"No," Ryan said immediately. "No, we are just friends, more like brother and sister."

"No girlfriend for you, then?"

"No. Maybe I'll find a gal when I get back." He shuffled his feet. It wasn't really a topic Ryan wanted to get into with his superior, mainly because everyone else he knew already had ladies of their own. Some of his friends were even married, but not him. He'd only had two girlfriends, and neither of those relationships lasted very long.

Ryan coughed to clear the tension in the air, then offered a polite "Sir!" and left the tent.

CHAPTER SIX

FIRST CALL TO ZALMA

EARTH–ZALMA BASECAMP, NEW MEXICO

Ryan had just finished packing when he received a summons on his communicator from Jones, requesting his presence on the bridge of the Ymit.

As Ryan entered, he noticed he was the last one to arrive. The general was already there, along with the three aliens he'd already met—Agugua, Edugra, Geogram—as well as a greenish Zalmen lady, and a slender soldier in his early thirties. Could these be the Cameron and Joanua that Donna had told him about?

Jones introduced them. "Ambassador Wilcox, meet Lieutenant Cameron and the Ymit's engineer, Joanua." He paused as Ryan first shook the slender man's hand and then exchanged bows with the engineer. "I've worked with Cameron for a long time. He is one of the best encryption specialists the army has to offer. While you've been negotiating, I've had Cameron learn their communications system from Joanua."

"A wise idea." Ryan took a moment to regard the two. His first impression was their calm manner. They didn't seem prone to outbursts of excitement like

Donna or Edugra, but they also didn't share the captain's seriousness. He nodded toward Joanua. "Thank you." Then Ryan turned to Cameron. "How did it go?"

"Great!" the lieutenant replied with a soft smile. "I had many ideas, and when you formalized the alliance, the ladies and I initiated implementation."

"So, what did you come up with?" Jones asked.

Cameron turned toward the main screens, which were lit up with multiple pages of code, in English. Ryan realized it had to be for Cameron's sake.

"First," Cameron said, "we tested routing low-powered directional signals through their probes in other solar systems. That way, the Moadites should not be able to track the source."

"Smart," Ryan said. *That sounds like the right thing to do.*

"Then I considered several of our encryption systems. The problem is that we can't transmit the encryption code to Zalma because anyone who intercepts it would also be able to decode our transmissions."

Jones shook his head, frowning. "And that's not good. So, what did you come up with?"

"We used a cipher key that only both sides have without transmitting. Since they have all their manuals and historical books electronically stored on the ship's computer, we coded a multibook cipher," Cameron explained.

"Multi-book!" Jones repeated. "Impressive!"

"Thank you, sir," the lieutenant said before he continued his explanation. He used his hands minimally as he spoke. "Once they have that, we will immediately send a secure transmission with more encryption algorithms. And, for really secure transmissions, the Zalmen can enter additional personal keys, like: *Where did we first meet?* With the Zalma super-fast computers, multi-layered secure communications are possible, and I am confident that the signals are secure."

"Wow!" Ryan said.

Cameron smiled. "The Zalmen are excited, as they haven't contacted their leaders and family since they left."

"Oh?" The general glanced around at the collected aliens.

With a start, Ryan realized that Kanara's family had snuck in some time during Cameron's explanation. He pulled his eyes away from them to look at Jones. "Yes," he said. "They told me that they sent brief automated messages that would look like one of their probes so the Moadites wouldn't pay any extra attention."

The older man hummed. "Good plan."

"With your and Captain Agugua's permission, sir, we are ready to start," Cameron said. When they both nodded, he and Joanua began uploading their files.

Ryan gaped at the glowing screens. It wasn't so much what was *on* the screens that impressed him—just loading bars and lines of code—but the appearance of the screen in general. The amazement he'd carried for the past few days of the Zalmen themselves had worn off a bit, but every time he looked at his communicator or anything else they'd brought with them, he couldn't stop his jaw from dropping. Vaguely, he registered Edugra's voice.

"The second probe has updated," she said. "Third…. Fourth…. Fifth…. Sixth…."

Ryan followed along, watching as lines of text changed on the screen.

"The seventh and final probe is now updated. We are transmitting encryption programs and terms of our alliance to Zalma," Edugra finished.

For the next few seconds, no one spoke. They waited with bated breath. Then the computer chimed, and a new rectangle popped up.

Edugra smiled. "Incoming coded transmission from Zalma!" she announced.

Everyone cheered. The humans exchanged handshakes. Edugra accepted the transmission. Sarara even clapped her hands together. The text vanished from the screen, and a live video transmission appeared.

Several Zalmen stared back at them through the screen with an assortment of blue, purple, and teal skin. All but one was dressed in silver robes.

Agugua bowed and spoke first—in Zalmen, which his communicator then translated to English for the humans. *"Council, I would like you to meet Ambassador*

Wilcox, General Jones, and Lieutenant Cameron." He pointed to each of them in turn. *"They are responsible for enabling us to communicate today."*

Ryan hastily bowed to the people on the screen in time with Jones and Cameron. He'd been distracted by studying the Zalman in the middle, the only one he'd ever seen wearing a different color. He wore a robe like the rest of the council, though his was a glossy white. He appeared to be Geogram's age, in his late fifties by human standards, though, unlike the ambassador, this Zalman was a much darker purple.

"I am First Minister Ronderra."

Ryan immediately noticed that his words didn't match the movement of his lips. He should've been used to this by now, but it seemed that the Zalmen would never cease to amaze him. *I bet the computer is translating right now for him.* Ryan remembered that when Agugua spoke, the computer translated, but the translation was delayed, until he stopped speaking. *I guess that's so it's not talking over him, and maybe it can do it in real time because we don't need to hear the original.* Ryan wasn't even sure that was possible—it wasn't something he'd ever considered—but the Zalmen were already doing much more than he'd ever imagined.

Ronderra continued, *"Thank you, gentlemen. We are grateful for your assistance. The deflectors are less effective than when our team left, and our timeline has been moved up. We believe the Moadites have new technology."*

As he spoke, a secondary image popped up, showing video footage of the planet's deflectors under enemy fire. One explosion, larger and brighter than any of the others, lit up across the screen. The entire Zalman sky flickered, casting spectral lights over the city buildings. Many of the Zalmen gasped, then breathed a sigh of relief when they saw what looked like the glass of a snow-globe rebuilding itself.

"We are glad to be of service," Jones said. "I'll be returning with your outreach team and with a small group of specialists to assess your needs."

Geogram stepped forward, bowing to the first minister. "I can vouch for General Jones's skill. He deduced our intentions from our decoy ship and its proximity to their nuclear test site. He and his team will be invaluable to us."

On the screen, the council members' colors flickered, and they murmured, clearly impressed.

Jones nodded, but otherwise showed no outward signs of acknowledgment. He remained calm and collected, entirely in his element. "The best course of action for now would be to begin analyzing the Moadite ships. We need to know what they're made of, and if they have deflectors. Would you be able to do that?"

"Yes, that is possible," Ronderra replied.

"Analyze their weapons as well," the general persisted. "I'd suggest launching rocks or metal debris into space and scanning the remains after they've been destroyed. If we can identify what types of weapons they're using, we might be able to modify your deflectors for better resistance."

The first minister's face flickered with green, then he nodded.

"Finally, we'd like you to record their ships' transmissions for us, so that we can have our decryption specialists take a look at them," Jones finished.

"We will do as you request," the first minister assured him.

Ryan, who'd been watching the exchange, felt a knot tighten in his gut as he realized just how far he had come, but how far he had to go to improve. The general spoke with such confidence. He simply said what he needed—he didn't ask. He didn't sound unsure, nor did he stumble over his words like Ryan knew he himself might've in front of so many older people.

One of the teal council members lifted a large communicator into view, taking the moment of silence as her cue to step forward. *"We are pleased with the success of the mission,"* she said first, then stared down at her communicator again. *"I see here that in exchange for human goods, we will be providing a station for your orbit."*

She looked up for confirmation, and Jones nodded.

"We have been preparing an invisible freighter for our new colony, but I believe our chances would be better if you use it as your space station. It has a large replicator and everything needed to start a space fleet."

"Thank you." The general acknowledged. He paused for a moment, then asked, "New colony?"

"Yes. In light of our weakening deflectors, we have been preparing to evacuate the planet." She'd barely gotten the words out before gasps erupted from the Ymit's crew members.

Ryan spun to see their colors fluctuating aggressively.

Jones spoke slower, with a deeper voice. "I'm sorry to hear that. I assure you we are doing everything we can to eliminate the need for evacuation."

"We had planned to use this ship as the base for our new colony," the teal council member maintained, *"but with your help, we hope we will not need it."*

"We look forward to these books and movies you are sending," a third Zalman added, *"both historical and artificial. They will be a welcome distraction to our people during these difficult times."* He gave a half-hearted smile.

I wonder if they'll ever get used to fiction, Ryan thought.

Next to him, Cameron mouthed, "Artificial?"

Ryan coughed lightly to cover a chuckle. "Fiction," he whispered.

Cameron chuckled as well.

"Well," Jones said, sending a quick frown in the two men's direction, "I am sure you have lots to talk about. We will leave you to it."

The three humans bowed.

Agugua turned to address his crew. "You may all contact your families now. I would recommend the privacy of your rooms."

Geogram stepped forward and spoke to the ministers in his own language.

The humans and remaining crew left the bridge.

CHAPTER SEVEN

PREPARING FOR THE SPACE FLIGHT

EARTH–ZALMA BASECAMP, NEW MEXICO

There was a rogue general, Scornson, interested in capturing or killing the aliens, so the base was moving to Area Three. The whole place was a flurry of chaos. All around Ryan, soldiers were packing bags, taking down tents, and loading supplies on the trucks. He carried two bags—his own and Donna's, but unlike the rest of the base residents, he and Donna weren't leaving on the truck; they were heading for the spaceship. Though the bags weren't heavy, he was light-headed and tired by the time he stepped through the phase variance.

Donna steadied him as he set down the luggage on the bridge. When he caught his breath and looked up, he noticed Geogram waiting for them. The ambassador greeted them both with a kind smile and a quick bow, which they returned.

After he and Ryan shook hands, Geogram wasted no time in leading them through the main door from the bridge and down a hallway. As Ryan stepped inside his room, his jaw nearly hit the floor.

"Holy mackerel!" Ryan cried. "You said you could duplicate our rooms, but this is identical to when we scanned it! Even my bedsheets are folded the same, and the garbage is full!"

Geogram stood perplexed, as he usually did, when it came to human interaction. "You sound surprised. I am sorry that the dimensions of the room are not exact. All the rooms are the same length, as is dictated by the distance from the hallway to the outer wall of the ship. We adjusted the width to give you almost the same amount of space."

"How can you make it so precise?" Ryan asked.

"Our nanite technology can duplicate anything." Geogram waved a hand carelessly around the room.

"Can it duplicate people?"

Geogram whitened. "No. Of course not. Why would you ask that?" He only relaxed when he heard Donna giggle from the doorway. "Oh…. Very funny! Should we make adjustments to the other rooms?"

"Just minor changes, I think. Definitely do *not* copy the garbage or dust." Ryan pointed to the bin. "Other than that, move the blankets a little or put the pen and paper in a slightly different spot. A little randomness makes us feel more relaxed."

"Why is that?"

"Good question. I'll let you know when I have a good answer." Ryan laughed, trying to show Geogram that he'd meant it as a joke, but the mauve alien stared at him blankly again. Ryan sighed. He'd gotten used to explaining things to the other ambassador over the past few days.

Donna spoke up. "Maybe it's because life's not perfect," she said. "And since we can't make it perfect, we'd rather not see anyone or anything that is."

Geogram nodded as if she'd just fed him one of the great mysteries of the universe. "Stimulating. Miss Warren, your room is next door." They dropped her luggage off in it. "Are you two ready for mealtime?"

"Dinner?" Ryan coached him on the English phrasing. Feeling the knot in his stomach, he replied, "Yes."

Heading back down the halls, the two humans admired the simplicity of the ship's design. Like a hotel, it had a single but wide straight hallway, well-lit, as the metal in the walls seemed to glow. Each doorway had a name on it. The names also glowed, like the door itself was a communicator. *Would they go through that expense to put communicators everywhere?*

Then they arrived at the dining room, where everyone else had already gathered for dinner. They were all sitting around a long rectangular table, strewn with serving platters of strange and colorful cubes.

The Zalmen had saved them seats in the middle. The ladies all sat across from the men, and the kids sat beside their parents. All the plates were already full and untouched; they'd been waiting.

"So, what is this?" Ryan asked, casting his eyes over the unfamiliar items.

He was surprised that Joanua, the engineer who was sitting next to Donna, spoke up. "Vegetables from our home planet," she said. "I ran numerous simulations to ensure they are compatible with your human biology." She seemed so proud of herself that Ryan nodded, though he was still apprehensive. "I also scanned the crops in your local farms to recreate flavors you would be familiar with. The white mound is similar to your potatoes. The green portion is like spinach, and the orange sticks and red cubes are like carrots and tomatoes."

"Wow!" Donna cried. "That sounds like a lot of work. Thank you so much."

Donna had already eaten a few bites and hadn't turned green, so Ryan risked a forkful of the colorful fair. He chewed, turning it over in his mouth. *Not bad matching the flavor,* he thought, but it was bland. Maybe they didn't believe in seasonings. "You did a great job. How did you do it?"

Joanua positively glowed, face filling with a burst of magenta. She was quick to contain herself and explain.

"I compared the chemical composition of your plants to ours. After performing a data matrix analysis, I was able to combine our plants in the right proportions to simulate the chemistry—and therefore the nutrition and flavor of your food."

"Would you happen to have scanned any seasonings, like salt or pepper?" His words were cautious as he realized he'd never actually seen the Zalmen eat. They were aliens; they probably had different taste buds.

Joanua frowned, though luckily, she didn't seem offended. "We have not found those plants yet."

"Oh…. Pepper is not grown locally. I can bring you some samples next time. And salt is not a plant; it's a mineral. We often dehydrate ocean water or mine it from the ground."

Around the table, the crew members were almost vibrating with how fast their colors changed. They were whispering too, and when Ryan strained to understand them, he found they weren't speaking English. Rather, their language reminded him of Mandarin and Navajo but was definitely different from either of them. Agugua was the closest and loudest, his words guttural, and all at once, Ryan could understand how the language gave him his accent.

Ryan looked across the table at Donna, who seemed similarly fascinated, though she tried to hide it by focusing on the food in front of her.

When the sound lulled, she took her chance. "The chemical compound for regular table salt is sodium chloride, if that helps."

"Ah, yes!" Joanua double tapped the table next to her plate, and a screen appeared in front of her. She input a few words, which Ryan guessed must've been the formula, because only a second later, a small container rolled out of a console in the wall and Joanua retrieved it for him. "Try this," she said.

Ryan shook the container. It sounded like salt, and when he peered inside, it looked and smelled like salt, too. He sprinkled it over the food and took a bite. "Much better! Thank you," he said. At least his food wouldn't be tasting like cardboard for the foreseeable future. *However,* he thought, *vegetables, no matter how seasoned they are, aren't a full meal.* He glanced around at the table, hoping to spot a steak or maybe even some chicken. When he found none, he frowned. "Where is the meat?"

The Zalmen blinked at him.

"What is meat? Your television showed these odd-shaped items on plates, but we were not able to identify them," Joanua said.

Ryan and Donna exchanged a look.

"They talked about chicken, which we identified as an animal that lays eggs, but in order to make the eggs that dark and hard, they must have really overcooked them."

His stomach dropped. How, in all these days of knowing each other, had he not thought to ask this? How could he have overlooked such a fundamental cultural difference? He'd dealt with different cultures before—humans had a lot of them, after all, and some were vegetarian, but not to this extent. Vegetarians on Earth at least knew what meat was. Ryan scolded himself, then carefully chose his next words. "Oh, you are vegetarian?"

"I don't know," Joanua replied. She seemed confused by the term; perhaps she'd never heard it before. "But we eat vegetables."

"I am sorry. How do I say this? Donna?" he turned to her, desperately searching for advice, but she shook her head. "OK, maybe we should talk about this later?"

Geogram leaned forward against the table, turning his body toward Ryan. "You have us all interested now. I think you should tell us."

"OK," Ryan said, squeezing his eyes shut for a long second. He took a deep breath. "This may come as a shock to you, so please hear me out, but when we talk about the *meat* from a chicken, we are not referring to the eggs. We are referring to...the...the... bird...itself."

No one spoke for a few seconds. Donna was stiff as a board across from him, and everyone else at the table had turned starched white like his words had turned them into ghosts. Edugra looked ready to jump up from her chair and bolt.

After a moment, the room seemed to explode with movement as flashes of red, yellow, white, and green filled Ryan's vision on all sides. The blood rushing in his ears subsided, only to be replaced by the racket of chatter from the crew members.

Geogram rose from his seat, deadly calm, and a hush fell over them. He stared down at Ryan, eyes hard as chips of stone. "Do we understand you correctly? You are saying that you eat the flesh of another living creature?"

"No," Ryan protested, "they are not living when—"

"How barbaric!" Edugra burst out. She stood up so quickly that her chair flew back, hit and absorbed into the wall. She stormed out of the room, followed quickly by Joanua, with Sarara and Kanara rushing Janara and Takar out.

Agugua set down his utensils and pointed at the humans. When he spoke through the translator, his words were quiet, though his voice shook with barely contained emotion. *You will leave,* he said. He pointed to himself and the other Zalmen. "We will discuss this."

I guess I should've expected this reaction. Ryan cursed himself—*I could've handled it better,* he thought—as he and Donna rose from their seats and headed for the hallway to their rooms. Geogram intercepted them with a raised hand, and Ryan almost flinched as he noticed that the other ambassador seemed afraid to touch him.

"I don't think you understand," Geogram said, pointing to the other side of the room, at another door Ryan didn't remember seeing before. "When Captain Agugua asked you to leave, he meant the ship."

Ryan's stomach dropped. The treaty, the alliance, Earth's first interstellar partnership, all crumbling because he'd mentioned meat. Donna's nails dug into his arm as the door hissed open to desert night.

Ryan lay awake that night, staring at the ceiling of his tent and replaying every moment of the failed dinner. Three days ago, he'd been proud of brokering humanity's first interstellar alliance. Now he wasn't sure if he'd just destroyed it over a chicken dinner.

Dad would have seen this coming. A real diplomat would have asked about their diet in the first five minutes.

CHAPTER EIGHT

BLUE MONDAY

EARTH–ZALMA BASECAMP, NEW MEXICO

Early on Monday morning, Ryan went to see the general. Jones had been discussing possible new recruits with Cpl. Dow, but turned his attention to Ryan as he entered. Thankfully, he didn't comment on Ryan's appearance as he hadn't slept well and probably looked as ragged as he felt.

"Ambassador." Jones's voice was neutral, not judging. "I hear things didn't go well on the weekend while I was away."

Ryan heaved a sigh, his face downcast. "No general, they did not! I goofed. Did you know that they're vegetarians? I mean, we should have guessed with the whole pacifist thing. They can't kill an animal to save their life, literally!"

"Oh, that is a problem," the general said. "I like my steak!"

"They called us barbaric and kicked us off the ship, then threw our luggage outside. I went back this morning to see if they were still there, but the door was closed. It's so weird. I can feel the doorway, but the rest of the ship isn't there. It's like they flew away without it!"

"The first time I entered the ship, they told me that it was in another dimension or something so it couldn't be detected, but they kept the door partially in our world so we can go in and out," Dow said.

"Is that even possible?" The question was rhetorical, but both young men shrugged anyway, and the general sighed. "Is there any *good* news?"

"Yes," Ryan replied. *And thank God for that.* "Donna has been talking to Edugra on her communicator. They've built up a friendship."

"And?"

"Donna prefers vegetarian food; she only eats meat when the people around her are. She has been sympathizing with them." The general gave Ryan a flat look, so he hurried on. "It turns out that all animals on Zalma are vegetarian. Sure, they eat eggs and drink milk, but no animal on their planet kills another. No animal eats another. They had no concept of what meat was."

"Well, now. I can see why they were so upset. That must have been quite a shock. What are you going to do about it?"

"What can I do?" Ryan asked. His tone bordered dangerously on a whine, so he pulled himself together. "They're not answering my calls, and I already told you the door's been closed since they kicked us out on Friday."

Dow chuckled. "How's that for timing?" he asked. "It's opening now."

The others turned to him. He hadn't moved, but he was looking at the side of the tent with interest.

"Zalma technology," the corporal explained, pointing at his glasses. "I can see heat through thin material—mostly a person's body heat. Someone is exiting the ship. Benjamin identifies him as Geogram, and he is heading this way."

"Benjamin?" Ryan found himself asking. The soldier had used that name before.

"That's what I decided to name my communicator," he replied.

Just then, Geogram entered the tent. He had a stiff posture and cold eyes. "Greetings. At the request of my daughter Edugra, I am inviting Ambassador Wilcox and Miss Warren back to the ship to talk. But there will be no—" he cleared his throat "—*dead animals* on board! Is that understood?"

It was the first time they heard Geogram speak with authority. Jones, Dow, and Ryan replied instinctively. "Yes, sir."

Geogram was taken aback but seemed pleasantly surprised with the response.

"Good. Ambassador, please retrieve your assistant so we may continue our discussions." Geogram headed back to the spaceship.

CHAPTER NINE

TENSIONS RUN HIGH

EARTH–ZALMA BASECAMP, NEW MEXICO

Ryan let out a sigh of relief as he stepped aboard the Ymit. They still had hope for the alliance to continue—if only they could figure out how to compromise. Other than the meat issue, the Zalmen had been entirely willing to provide them with whatever they needed.

"We do hope that our work together may continue without trouble or delay," Geogram said.

Ryan's grip tightened on the communicator in his hand. He'd just reviewed the list of requests from the general's team members, but having the device in his hand was comforting. "I agree, so let's get started. Our warriors are very physical people, and they need a lot of space to exercise and play games to stay strong."

Geogram nodded. He folded his hands together. "How much room will they require?"

"Honestly, as much room as you can give them. One wants a jogging track, one wants a weightlifting room, and another wants a target range, but they all want to play sports, like baseball, basketball, and football."

Captain Agugua turned around in his chair and spoke in Zalmen. *"Do they need a different room for each sport?"* the computer translated.

"No," Ryan said. "One room, a gymnasium, can accommodate everything. We would just have to move and store the goalposts, basketball hoops, and targets. You may have seen these sports on television."

Joanua displayed an outline of the ship (one long strip with a hallway on one side, and rooms on the other) on the main screen.

"Yes, I like your baseball. It is the least violent of them all," Agugua said through the translator. *"Kanara's daughter enjoyed it greatly when she played."*

Edugra clapped her hands together cheerfully. "I remember seeing those sports," she remarked. "The fields were similar in length to our ship but twice the width." She found several sports fields and laid an outline of them on the main screen over top of the ship's blueprint.

"We were planning to build a second floor for the human rooms, but instead we could put them on the main level and build the second floor for the sports." Joanua typed something, and the main screen updated with the new layouts. She looked at the captain for authorization.

Agugua nodded.

Joanua nodded back. "I will enter the specifications of the extra crew quarters and gymnasium into the ship's computer. With our nanite technology, it should only take a day for the additional rooms to grow onto the ship."

"If the gymnasium is on the top, can you put lots of windows on the walls and ceiling? That would make a great view," Donna said.

"I can make all the ceiling and walls transparent," Joanua said.

"Won't that be dangerous? Couldn't the glass break?" Ryan asked.

Joanua shook her head. "No. The transparent material will not be made from your glass; it is indeed much stronger than glass. Our deflectors will also stop anything from breaking it."

Everyone seemed satisfied, so Joanua proceeded. "General Jones requested replica phones so you can call home at any time. While the space transmission is crystal clear, we have created the option to add static to sound like your mobile radiophone, for when you are calling family from space."

"Great! Thank you." Ryan smiled. "Now I think it's time Ambassador Geogram and I talk in private."

Leaving the others to their work, Ryan followed the other ambassador from the bridge to a small conference room. He took one of the chairs around the table, sitting across from Geogram. He knew he had to speak quickly, to give Geogram the information he needed to make an informed decision, so he didn't wait for pleasantries; he just jumped right into their discussion.

"Donna and I are willing to switch to vegetarian," he offered, "but our warriors need meat to keep up their strength. We're willing to bring our own supply; we just need a place to keep it frozen."

"No. Absolutely not," Geogram said firmly, hand in the air. "No dead animals on our ship, and especially not on our home planet. It goes against everything that we believe in."

Ryan was at a loss for what to do. The other ambassador had left no room for discussion, and if he'd been a more desperate man, he'd have pleaded with the alien to understand. He opened his mouth to speak several times, but nothing came out. As a man of business—a negotiator—he would *not* make a deal that was not equal. "Sorry, but our warriors won't go without it."

Geogram turned yellow but remained silent.

Ryan took that as his cue to continue. "My people are already giving up a lot so they can help you. Think about it. They are voluntarily leaving their homes, everything and everyone they know, to go into space and defend a planet that they just heard about a week ago. *Your* planet! And you want them to give up their diet too? That would not be healthy for them. They'll be no use to you if they're too weak to fight or focus."

Parts of the yellow deepened to green, leaving his skin a mottled canvas. "I have spoken to First Minister Ronderra and the council, and they have made their decision. If you intend to bring dead animals upon the ship, they will not allow you aboard. It is barbaric. That is all to be said; we will not change our minds."

"So that's it?" Ryan shot to his feet. That ugly feeling that had been settling deep in his gut for the past few days had suddenly bubbled up into rage. "You know, you are the most selfish, uncompromising species I have ever known. You spy on other planets and don't see anything wrong with it."

"We are *not* spies," Geogram snapped, flashing yellow. "We are trying to protect ourselves."

"No. What you're doing is putting everyone else at a disadvantage by watching and recording their every move. And what's worse, you've been transmitting our broadcasts out into space, where anyone could intercept them and find out where we are! What if they decided to invade us next because of what we have?"

"The Moadites are far past your technology. They will not attack you for it."

Ryan snarled. "I'm sure it all makes perfect sense to you. You don't even see how what you're doing could affect others! You use your technology to gain information about us humans and the Moadites without consent. How would you feel if the roles were reversed? How would you like to be watched?"

Geogram didn't respond. His yellow skin flashed several different colors, including scarlet, orange, and indigo. His lips remained firmly closed, eyes watching Ryan's face. That only angered the human more.

"Maybe if we were watching you, we would find out who was teaching you this technology. You never did answer that question. You keep your secrets, but act like you're entitled to the secrets of everyone else." He growled.

Geogram held his gaze angrily but still refused to say anything.

How could he just look back at him like he didn't need to explain his actions? *How can he think what his people are doing is OK?* "And the Moadites are angry with you for it. They want you to stop spying on them. Why should we get involved? You deserve their wrath.

"We have been at a disadvantage from the start. If you didn't offer to exchange technology with us, we would have no reason to help you. Maybe you should just leave and deal with the Moadites yourself."

At last, Ryan couldn't take it anymore. He wished an outside door would appear again, or that he was closer to the exit as he stormed out of the conference room and down the hall. He was sure he'd get back to the bridge and off the ship before Geogram followed, but he was wrong. The purple alien was on his tail.

"But then you will have no way to defend Earth when the Moadites come," Geogram pointed out.

It was a good thing that the hallway was empty because Ryan wasn't sure he wanted any of the ladies to hear if he finally did lose his temper. "What would they want from us? You said it yourself: we don't have any technology. We didn't spy on them. We are no threat to them. So please, give me one good reason I shouldn't recommend the termination of this alliance right now." He spun around to face Geogram, only to pause in surprise when he saw that the alien's face was completely white. He was afraid. *Why?*

"The council does not accept the eating of meat because our people need to be reassured. If you kill other animals for food, what is to stop your people from doing the same to us?"

"*You think that we would—*" Ryan choked on the words. "I can't even say it. We are not *monsters*! If that's what you think of us, then obviously this alliance isn't going to work. We were willing to compromise, but you don't even know the meaning of the word. Call me when you've decided to be more cooperative." With that said, he whirled back around and stomped the rest of the way off the ship.

Ryan shook with nerves by the time he entered the soldiers' barracks. Gen. Jones had called a meeting with the whole team as if they were still going to space, but he wasn't even sure if the alliance was still happening after that last big argument that he'd had with Geogram.

He glanced at the men. It was an odd, mixed

group—a pilot, a marine, an engineer, and a communications expert. He'd met a few of them recently, and could link names to faces, but other than that, all of them were strangers.

Jones introduced Ryan to the men.

"We've recently learned that there are no carnivores on Zalma. None whatsoever on the whole planet." Ryan paused, waiting for a reaction, but the men were silent. He felt his heart throbbing under their watchful eyes. "That means they've never heard of one animal eating another. They were horrified to hear that we do it all the time."

"What that means for *us*," Jones said, stepping in, "is that they won't allow us to bring meat onto the ship."

A chorus of groans rose from the assembled men, though none voiced complaints yet, so Ryan forged ahead.

"I am sorry, I have been trying to negotiate a compromise...but the Zalmen are strict vegetarians and *very* set in their beliefs. I'm afraid the ladies might spew if I even bring up the topic when they're around."

Sergeant Bruno Abbott stood first. A soldier in mind and body, Ryan was sure the man could probably pop his head right off his shoulders.

"If that's the case, I'm not going!" Abbott declared. "No meat, no marine! The president isn't ordering us out...right, general?"

"Correct," Jones admitted—reluctantly. "This is a voluntary mission."

"This is the chance of a lifetime. Think of the technology we will gain," Ryan interjected, hoping he could turn this around.

Abbott spat into the dirt. "I don't care about technology. I'm a soldier! I say you're just whistlin' dixie with these chromedome aliens. Oddballs, all of them. Who doesn't eat *meat*?"

Ryan sputtered, but then Brian Howard, a civilian weapons designer, spoke up. "Well, I *am* interested in their technology. I could try going vegetarian, but I don't know how long I would last."

Of *course* he'd be interested in the science. "The good news is that they have expanded their garden so we can have our fresh fruit and vegetables, and they are willing to make room for the general's personal chef."

"That'd be better than any field ration kit, but...he can only cook vegetarian?" asked Lieutenant Colin McKenzie, a pilot.

More protests arose from the group, but Jones lifted a hand, and they all fell silent. "Wilcox, you've got one day to work things out, or the president's likely to pull the plug on this whole thing, and you know he'll do it. He's been clear in his opinion of this from the start. Dismissed!"

Ryan gulped. He was no stranger to the president's views of the aliens. He wasn't against them, but he certainly wasn't enthusiastic about the alliance. Sure, he'd been interested in the weapons, but the loss of his best general wasn't the most ideal situation.

The others followed as Jones left the barracks, getting back to their daily activities.

Ryan watched as Abbott returned to training with the other soldiers. They were running intensive drills, and Ryan's body ached just watching them.

He thought again of eating a strict vegetarian diet, and his stomach flipped over. It just…didn't seem possible. Abbott was fit, and the way he lived was vital to that. Ryan couldn't imagine him completely switching his diet without adverse effects on his health.

Some time later, Ryan's communicator chirped in his pocket. When he answered, Edugra's face stared up at him.

"Can we meet?" she asked.

"Sure, I'll be right there."

A few minutes later, he entered her room on the Ymit, finding Donna and Joanua already in there with her. *What's this all about?* He glanced at his assistant with the question in his eyes.

Edugra signaled him to come in all the way so the door would close. She shook, and her color changed repeatedly through the whole range, including blue, green, red, purple, and white. "I am sorry," she said. "I know you two are doing your best to find a solution to this problem."

"Thank you." He was still confused, but the sincerity in her voice was touching.

"I do have to say that when I went to your mess hall, the smell nearly made me vomit, and I had to leave."

"Many humans enjoy the smell of cooked meat," Ryan said. "I know you find that hard to believe, but it's true."

"Is there any way you can convince your people that they do not need meat?"

"No—because it's not the truth. Once your body is accustomed to a certain diet, changing it often has many unwanted side effects."

Edugra turned blue, and she nodded slowly. "I had hoped for some sort of compromise, but it is not my place to make those decisions. Your scientists have already helped strengthen our deflectors. Our leaders believe that it will hold the Moadites off long enough for them to evacuate the planet." Her voice grew smaller. "If you cannot come up with a compromise, we are to leave," she whispered.

"Are you saying that they are taking the help we gave them and then dumping us?" Ryan asked. "That's not fair."

Edugra nodded. "I know. I am similarly distressed. Our crew members have enjoyed spending time with you humans. I do not believe that it is fair for my people to do such a thing."

"It *is* unfair," Joanua said firmly. She reached out to put her hand on Edugra's shoulder. "Sarara, Kanara, and I have been bonding with you humans as well. I especially have been impressed by how much I am learning about creativity." She looked at the two humans. "You are an unusual but interesting species."

Donna, who hadn't spoken the whole time, giggled at Joanua's words. "Well...thanks!" she seemed hopeful to lift the gloomy mood.

Ryan realized Donna was only there to provide moral support for Edugra as she shared this information with him.

"Our soldiers aren't budging," Ryan said the next time he and Donna entered the bridge. He glanced around at the entire crew. "They will not go without meat."

Geogram sniffed pointedly, his nose high in the air and his skin dark red. "Our council has expressed their objection to your barbaric practices. If you will not give them up, they have called an end to our alliance. They would rather see how they fare with the Moadites."

"What if we found new warriors? Ones who are already vegetarian?" Donna asked. Her own face was flushed with emotion.

It was a last second attempt, and Ryan was annoyed she hadn't discussed it with him first, but he appreciated her effort.

"We would accept that," Geogram said. "How long would that take?"

"Well, there are some Eastern cultures that are vegetarian," Ryan said. He hummed as he made the mental calculations. "We would have to accelerate foreign recruitment and then train them. Maybe a year?"

Geogram frowned, shaking his head. He turned away. "Then you can keep your communicator, and if you come up with something else, you can give us a call."

CHAPTER TEN

THE END OF THE ALLIANCE

EARTH–ZALMA BASECAMP, NEW MEXICO

Ryan had been given this mission—straight from the president's mouth—barely a week ago, and it had already fallen apart. He had failed!

He let out a sigh as the crew members on the bridge sent them off.

Agugua, as the captain, approached them first with a polite bow. *"Thank you for trying,"* he said through the translator. *"We will miss you."*

Donna shook the captain's hand.

Ryan followed behind her, shaking Joanua, Kanara, Sarara, Janara, and Takar's hands.

Donna threw herself at Edugra, pulling her friend into a tight hug.

"Keep your communicator close," Edugra said.

"I will," Donna replied. "We can still chat, right?"

Edugra nodded, then turned to Ryan. "This is a shame," she said, her face downcast and washed with red. "I was looking forward to working with you more."

He smiled back at her sadly. A strange feeling was welling up in his chest. For a moment he wondered if he was having a heart attack, but then disregarded it as disappointment in his failure. "I'll miss you, too." Then he turned to the last member.

Geogram was as put together as always, his posture rigid and his chin held high. "Ambassador," he said formally, offering a quick bow.

It was shallower than when he'd first greeted them. Nonetheless, Ryan returned it. "Ambassador," he acknowledged. Then he stepped off the ship.

A moment later, Donna was next to him, and when they turned, nothing but desert spread out before them. He cautiously reached out a hand, but the ship was gone.

Gen. Jones summoned them to his tent. Ryan *really* wasn't in the mood, but Donna's insistence had convinced him to follow his superior's orders.

"You did an incredible job," the general offered in comfort.

Ryan looked away. "Thank you, sir. I just—"

"It was *not* your fault, son," Jones said firmly, cutting off his protests. "You did everything you could. The president and I want you to know that we are very proud of you."

Ryan replied with a smile. He knew the general's words were only half-right. The president wouldn't have said that. He'd made himself clear what a great waste of time this alliance was. Sure, he'd be happy to take credit for it if the mission had been a success, but it wasn't. He could hardly expect the president to be happy with his actions. "Thank you, sir," he said all the same.

Donna leaned over the back of Ryan's chair before settling in the one next to him. She, too, looked forlorn. "It would've been sweet to go into space, but I guess it wasn't in the cards. How did we even start working with aliens in the first place? I doubt they flew right up to the White House to talk to the president."

Cpl. Dow grinned cheekily at Cpl. Rabinowitz. "I was the first human to meet them, actually."

"How'd that happen?" She stared at the corporal with wide, curious eyes. The corners of her lips were upturned with interest.

Rabinowitz spoke before Dow got a chance. "Our detachment was called in to clean up a crash site near Roswell."

Dow cut in. "They thought it was a supply container or something, but it was a spaceship, like a lifeboat. Inside, we saw three dead aliens."

Ryan frowned. "You never mentioned anything about *dead* aliens before."

Dow chuckled. "Oh, the aliens in the ship were dummies. They wanted to test our reactions."

This time Rabinowitz cut in. "After that, we met the *real* alien, Geogram. He asked for our help to contact the government, and from there, I sought out General Jones."

"Yes. I was the commander of the base and was called to inspect the wreckage. The proximity to the nuclear test site had me concerned, until I realized that it looked more like a refugee situation than a military one. When Dow and Rabinowitz showed up, they confirmed my suspicions."

Ryan raised his eyebrows. "So, how'd you figure it out? Was it because the dummies were fake?"

Jones shook his head. "No, they were quite real. I had the local veterinarian do an autopsy on the alien bodies, and the doctor said that while he had never seen anything like them, their bodies reminded him of a stillborn calf."

Rabinowitz nodded. "Geogram told us that they're genetically modified clones."

"Cloning?" Donna repeated, disbelieving. "As in the novel, *A Brave New World*? Creating two identical beings?"

"Yeah, that's it. You read it too?"

"They were very convincing clones," the general explained. "The doctor who performed the autopsies believed they were real, but he didn't know how they died."

"Did you ever find out?" she asked.

Ryan could tell that Donna was itching for a notepad. *A Brave New World* had been one of her favorite novels back when they both read it.

"They were never alive," Dow explained. "They were grown in a lab like plants."

That comment made Ryan pause. "*Wait?* They just grew a *body?*" He paused. "What if they could grow other animals, like a cow?" He trailed off, his mind whirring with possibilities.

"Oh my God!" Jones shouted; his eyes were wide as saucers. "How did we miss this? Do you think it would work?"

"Do you think *what* would work?" Dow asked, staring between both of them in confusion. "What are you talking about? Did I miss something?"

Ryan turned to him. "The Zalmen are against us *killing* animals to eat them. But they eat eggs, which are also animals, just that they were never alive to begin with. Would they still be against us eating meat if it was never alive either?"

CHAPTER ELEVEN

A NEW HOPE

After Ryan finished his *very* long call to Geogram, he was sure he'd run out of breath. The alien ambassador, of course, had been skeptical from the moment Ryan called. Perhaps it had something to do with how quickly he'd called after they left.

But once Ryan told him their plan, Geogram's rough edges softened. He seemed pleased that Ryan had figured out a solution for them that didn't force them to give up their practices. He'd called Joanua to see if it was possible.

After talking back and forth, they'd *finally* come to an agreement.

He put the communicator in his pocket and looked over at Donna. She was staring back at him, as quiet as she'd been during the call, but now she was smiling.

When they joined Gen. Jones, Cpl. Dow, and Cpl. Rabinowitz outside, they were standing at the edge of camp, staring up at the cloudless sky. They seemed to be waiting for something.

"So, what did they say?" the general asked.

He hadn't turned, so obviously, he'd heard the crunching of Ryan's footsteps on the dry Earth. "Geogram doesn't see a problem with us eating cloned meat on board the ship. He suspects that the council will stipulate that you do not eat meat in public on Zalma, or discuss meat with any Zalmen. He's concerned that if their people saw meat, even cloned, they would wonder what it is, and the answer would cause the same fear that they experienced at our first meal, and he doesn't want his people to be afraid of us. He told me he'd discuss it with their council and see if they felt the same. Then, he'll let us know."

Dow nodded, then turned away from the sky and rubbed at his eyes.

"Care to finish your stories?" Donna asked.

The general and the two corporals took turns telling their stories. When they were finished, they looked up.

"I don't know why we are looking!" Dow protested. "I have never seen their ship; it's always invisible. Have any of you seen it?" He looked at the others.

Everyone shook their heads.

Ryan was hungry, as he hadn't eaten all day. He took Donna for dinner, and when they came back, the sun was painting the sky in peachy oranges. Soon they were staring up at the dark sky, waiting for something to happen.

Nothing did.

Dow sighed. "Well, I guess they're not coming back," he said. "You'd think that they could have at least called." With a huff, he hauled himself up off the ground where he'd been lying and was just about to head back to his own tent for the night when something finally changed.

A song was playing, coming from an unseen source. Ryan peered into the distance. There was something shining in the sky. At first, he'd thought it was just a star, but it was getting bigger. The song was growing louder.

The star was soon too big to be a star, and Ryan saw the Ymit for the first time. It was a massive flying rectangle, descending from the darkening sky. The outside gleamed silver, reflective, and shiny.

"How does that thing even fly? It doesn't look aerodynamic whatsoever," Ryan said.

"If they can make it invisible, control gravity, and grow clones, I think they can make a shoebox fly," Dow replied.

Ryan nodded. Now that the ship was in sight, he could hear the familiar song's lyrics.

"'You Are My Sunshine'!" Donna shouted excitedly. "That's Ryan's and my favorite song!"

"Wow, it's huge!" Dow shouted, completely ignoring Donna.

After hearing the song and seeing the ship, Ryan thought the display couldn't get any flashier, but he was wrong. Small projectiles shot out from the ship and into the sky, exploding in a burst of sparks and color. Pops and bangs filled the air, jolting the entire basecamp of Area Three.

A dozen other recruits ran out of their tents, some holding their rifles, ready to fight off the invading forces, but then they looked up, and their jaws dropped.

As the first round of fireworks cleared, another song played, this time, smooth jazz.

Jones hummed. "'Sentimental Journey'. That's *my* favorite." He sounded pleased. "And would you look at that display! They must be learning imagination." Then he chuckled, looking around at the looks of awe on the soldiers' and civilians' faces. "It's a good thing we're the only ones around for miles out here in the desert."

A second round of fireworks began. It opened with a shower of gold, then stars of blue and red. The sky, once painted by the sunset, was awash with more colors than Ryan could've imagined. All too soon, the fireworks were over, a third song, an upbeat tune on a trumpet, began to play.

"'Boogie Woogie Bugle Boy'," Dow identified. "That's the one *I* told Joanua about."

They listened with wide grins on their faces, and as the song ended, a third display of lights filled the night sky around the hovering ship. Then it descended the rest of the way and touched down on the empty desert.

A door opened, and in the distance, Ryan could see the aliens walking toward them. He waved. "That was quite an entrance!" he called as they got closer.

Geogram nodded politely, sending a quick smile at his daughter, and Ryan *knew* it must've been her idea. "We observed your Fourth of July celebrations before we sent the decoy and based it on that. Did we get it right?"

Ryan was grinning ear to ear. "Yes, I'd say so!" He found that, in the rush of emotions, he didn't care that the alliance had almost failed. All he could think about was that the Zalmen had returned.

DID YOU ENJOY THIS BOOK?

Your feedback helps me provide the best quality books and helps other readers like you discover them.

It would mean the world to me if you took two minutes to share your thoughts about this book. You can leave a review with the retailer of your choice and/or send an email to *tony@tonybrichard.com* with your honest feedback.

Thank you, I really appreciate it.

ACKNOWLEDGMENTS

As always, thanks to all who have helped make these books happen. My beta readers and critique group. Alex Perkins for his cover work. Carolin Petersen for putting it all together.

Also, a special thanks to all those who write positive and encouraging stories, both in books and on TV.

PRONUNCIATIONS

Ymit	YEM—it
Geogram	Ge—OG—ram
Agugua	A—GU—gwa
Joanua	Jo—ANN—wa
Edugra	Ed—oog—RA
Sarara	Sa—RARE—ah
Kanara	Can—AR—ah
Ronderra	Ron—der—RAH
Zalma	ZALL—mah
Zalmen	ZALL—men
Moad	Moe—ADD
Moadites	Moe—ADD—eytes

SERIES TIMELINE

ROSWELL: FIRST CONTACT
Malcolm Dow & Adam Rabinowitz: Episode 1

NEGOTIATIONS
Ryan Wilcox: Episode 1

THE GOOD, THE BAD, AND THE UNDECIDED
Greg Newman: Episode 1

DEFYING GRAVITY
Mary Goss: Episode 1

(spanning the entire timeline)

CHARLIE'S BIG CHANCE   THE WOUNDLESS WAR
Charlie Baker: Episode 1   *Frank Jones: Episode 1*

FROM ROSWELL TO AREA 51: THE NOVEL
(a single "cinematic cut" that braids all six POVs in chronological order)

Earth's Secret Alliance is a series of clean,
family friendly, uplifting,
one-to-two-hour short stories.

ROSWELL: FIRST CONTACT

When Private Malcolm Dow went to clean up a crashed weather balloon, hey came face-to-face with an alien instead.

Adam Rabinowitz was one of those wimps who followed Dow around, hoping for protection from the bullies.

While Dow was reluctant, Rabinowitz instantly took on the Alien's plight – military help for his besieged planet, Zalma. But when he gets caught, it's up to Dow to save the day.

If they fail, it's not just Zalma; Earth may be captured or destroyed next. But if they are to succeed, they must work around the chain of command to avoid the anti-alien majority.

THE GOOD, THE BAD, AND THE UNDECIDED

Major General Greg Newman has always been self-centered and opportunistic-even using WWII as a stepping stone to advance his career. Now that the war is over, he's looking for a new way to add more stars to his shoulders. Soon Greg is approached about a secret mission spying on a superior officer and a classified research facility. He hopes this job will land him that quick promotion but has reservations about surveilling this officer. Voicing his concern is only met with not-so-subtle threats.

Now entangled in a diabolical plan, Greg questions which boundaries he's unwilling to cross. If he doesn't jettison his morals entirely, then his career will surely go down in flames. Greg must decide who to trust, and that becomes a choice between a quick promotion, or saving his country—and maybe even the world.

DEFYING GRAVITY

In 1947, there's an alien invasion looming and humankind's best hope is a brilliant nineteen-year-old woman.

When the A-bomb ended the war, with a power unlike anything humans had ever witnessed, Mary Goss was driven to gain the knowledge to prevent another war from ever beginning. Now the Army has come calling, looking for "a few good men" for a top-secret project. Instead, they find that the best and brightest is Mary.

Much to Mary's horror, the project reveals an alien invasion. Yet at every turn, her efforts to intervene are thwarted by small-minded engineers who can't look past her gender and age. She'd dealt with her fair share of discrimination in university, but with the fate of the world on the line, there isn't time to waste on petty differences.

CHARLIE'S BIG CHANCE

Aliens. A notebook. A secret no one will believe.

Charlie Baker is 12 years old, dreams of being a reporter, and uses a wheelchair to get around her small town. When she stumbles across a crashed alien ship near Roswell, everything changes.

Now Charlie has a chance to write the story of a lifetime—but telling the truth might put the aliens in danger. Can she keep their secret, even as the military closes in?

THE WOUNDLESS WAR

In 1947, a UFO crash-lands in Roswell, New Mexico, bringing General Frank Jones face to face with the alien Zalmen. Desperate for help, the Zalmen reveal their advanced technology, but with a catch: they are pacifists, and will only allow Frank to use it if he doesn't kill anyone. As the clock ticks down and the enemy Moad close in, Frank must find a way to save the Zalmen and their planet without taking any lives. But if he fails, the Moad will use the Zalmen's technology against Earth, with devastating consequences.

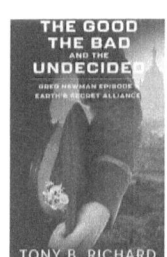

ABOUT THE AUTHOR

Tony B. Richard lives in Langley, British Columbia. He is a computer programmer (coder) and instructor. This grand adventure has been in his head for decades, and during the Covid-19 pandemic, he thought it was finally time to put it down on paper.

"Differences are something to be celebrated, not feared."
—TONY B. RICHARD

YOU CAN CONTACT HIM WITH QUESTIONS OR COMMENTS AT:

Website: www.tonybrichard.com
Email: tony@tonybrichard.com
Facebook: EarthsSecretAlliance
Twitter: @TonyBRichard1
Instagram: tony_b_richard
Goodreads: Tony B. Richard